One Up, One Down

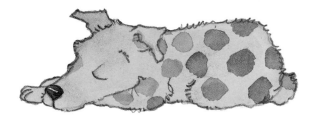

Atheneum Books for Young Readers

One Up,

One Down

Carol Snyder **illustrated by Maxie Chambliss**

Atheneum Books for Young Readers
Simon & Schuster Children's Publishing Division
1230 Avenue of the Americas
New York, New York 10020

Book design by Kimberly M. Adlerman
The text is set in 18-point Times Roman.
The illustrations are rendered in watercolor.
First edition
Printed in the United States of America
10   9   8   7   6   5   4   3   2   1

Library of Congress Cataloging-in-Publication Data
Snyder, Carol.
One up, one down / by Carol Snyder; illustrated by Maxie
Chambliss.—1st ed.
p.   cm.
Summary: Katie is so busy helping to take care of her new twin
brothers she does not notice that she has grown as well.
ISBN 0-689-31828-6
[1. Twins—Fiction.   2. Babies—Fiction.   3. Brothers and sisters—
Fiction.]   I. Chambliss, Maxie, ill.   II. Title.
PZ7.S68517On   1995
[E]—dc20   93-36282

To all miracle babies, especially twins:
Adam and Ben
Alyssa and Nicole
with special thanks to all big brothers and sisters
—C. S.

For Erik and Ryan Robertson Wilke:
One up, one down
with love all around
—M. C.

"It's time," Mommy said.

Grandma came to stay with me. Then Mommy and Daddy left in a hurry.

Ben

Adam

"Surprise!" Daddy said early the next morning. "You have *two* baby brothers—twins."

"No wonder Mommy was so fat," I said.

"You'll be a big help to us, Katie," Daddy said. "How does it feel to be a big sister?" he asked.

I looked in the mirror. Same size as always.

Adam and Ben were tiny at first. And although they were twins, they were not at all alike. Curly hair and straight. Dark hair and light. If Adam was up at night, Ben was asleep. Then as soon as Adam settled down, Ben was up screaming.

Ben   Adam

"One up. One down. One wet. One dry." I yawned and handed Daddy a diaper. We were all very sleepy.

Every week Ben and Adam got a little bigger. Every week
Mommy and Daddy said, "Katie, you are a good big sister."

Every week I looked in the mirror. Same size as always.

At feeding time, if Ben was propped up, Adam would slide down and I'd fix him.

But by the time Adam was propped up, Ben slipped down and was crying.

"One up. One down," I said, and handed Mommy a bottle.

Soon both babies sat up just fine. And I gave them each a rattle. If Ben held his rattle up, Adam dropped his on the ground.

If Adam's rattle was up, Ben's was down.
"One up. One down,"
I said. We all got lots of exercise.

Then they got their first tooth. Adam's was on the top. Ben's was on the bottom. As I fed mashed banana to Adam and said, "Swallow it down," Ben would spit up his. We all wore drips of cereal and fruit.

Soon both babies slept all night through. And sat up straight.
And held their rattles.

And soon the twins could stand and take walks around the house. I'd hold each one's hand. But when Adam walked nicely, Ben *kerplunk!* sat down. And just as I got Ben up...

"One up. One down."
"You're one tired big sister, aren't you," Daddy said.
I looked in the mirror. Tired and the same size as always.

When Adam and Ben discovered the stairs, Adam loved to creep up. Ben loved to scoot down. We all had backaches from the bending.

When we took them to the playground, Adam tried to crawl up
the baby slide just as Ben slid down. I stopped them just in time.
We all had headaches from the crying.

Adam spoke his first two words. "One up," he said.
"One down," said Ben.
"That's for sure," I said.

One day we took them to the shoe store for their first pair of shoes. "Better check Katie's shoes, too," Daddy said. And the shoe store lady measured my foot.

Ben's and Adam's shoes had laces, but I got new shoes with buckles. I looked in the mirror.

My feet were bigger than always. I was taller than always (even if I was more tired than always).

"Now I feel like a big sister," I said.

"And a helpful one, too," said Mommy.

"One up," said Adam as he held his foot up in the air.
"One down," I said as Ben sat down and put his in his mouth.

MY THANKS TO AMY SNYDER, ED. M., FOR HER EXPERT ADVICE